A Rattle of Bones

A Halloween Book of Collective Nouns

by Kipling West

Orchard Books : New York

To Alan Haynes, who likes Halloween as much as I do

The terms "a put-on of costumes," "a leer of jack-o'-lanterns," "a tribe of trick-or-treaters," "a gabble of goblins," "a bridge of trolls," "a grimace of masks," and "a rattle of bones" are from *An Exaltation of Home and Family* by James Lipton, copyright © 1993 by James Lipton, and are reprinted by permission of Villard Books, a division of Random House.

The terms "a cackle of hyenas," "a venom of spiders," and "a wake of vultures" are from *An Exaltation of Larks* by James Lipton, copyright © 1968, 1977, 1991 by James Lipton, and are reprinted by permission of Viking Penguin, a division of Penguin Putnam Inc.

Orchard Books, A Grolier Company, 95 Madison Avenue, New York, NY 10016

Manufactured in the United States of America. Printed and bound by Phoenix Color Corp.
Book design by Mina Greenstein. The text of this book is set in 22 point Jacoby Black.
The illustrations are ink and acrylic paintings.   10   9   8   7   6   5   4   3   2   1

Library of Congress Cataloging-in-Publication Data
West, Kipling. A rattle of bones : a Halloween book of collective nouns / by Kipling West.
p.   cm. Summary: An assortment of collective nouns are revealed as some
children go out on Halloween night.
ISBN 0-531-30196-6 (trade : alk. paper).—ISBN 0-531-33196-2 (library : alk. paper)
[1. Halloween—Fiction. 2. Stories in rhyme.] I. Title.
PZ8.3.W49975Rat   1999   [E]—dc21   99-12618

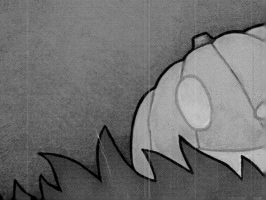

a GRIMACE of masks

a LEER of Jack-o'-lanterns

and meet our friends beneath the stars.

a TRIBE of trick-or-treaters

a GABBLE of goblins

The smallest monsters prowl tonight,

a BRIDGE of trolls

a MURDER of crows

a PRESS of ghosts

The night is dark—we've lost our way

a RATTLE of bones

a GLARING of cats

among the trees where creatures roam.

a KINDLE of kittens

a VENOM of spiders

Through the dark and scary wood
will we find a safe way home?

a WAKE of vultures

an UNKINDNESS of ravens

Who is that? Friend or foe?

a PARLIAMENT of owls

a CONSTELLATION of stars

Here is someone who will know.

a CAN of worms

a DIVERSITY of creatures

a CACKLE of hyenas

We'll dance and laugh and sing and cheer.

a FLOAT of dancers

Home is not so far from here.

a COLONY of frogs

The moon looks in to say good night
when we're in bed tucked in tight,
dreaming of friends who'll stay unseen
till the moon shines bright next Halloween.

Author's Note

Believe it or not, the word for a group of ravens really is an "unkindness." Just as a group of crows is called a "murder." While these two words have been around for many years, some of the terms in this book are much newer. Whether it was hundreds of years ago or only last week, someone made up these words to describe groups of things.

All of the terms in *A Rattle of Bones* appear in previously published sources, including *An Exaltation of Larks* (New York: Viking, 1991) and *An Exaltation of Home and Family* (New York: Random House, 1993), both by James Lipton; *A Dictionary of Collective Nouns and Group Terms* by Ivan Sparkes (Detroit: Gale Research Co., 1985); and *The World Almanac and Book of Facts* by Robert Famighetti (New York: St. Martin's Press, 1995). But collective nouns don't have to be from an "official" source like the dictionary or encyclopedia in order to be valid. If you like the words in this book, try to make up some of your own! What would you call a group of math teachers, for example? Or how about a group of bratty younger brothers and sisters? Use your imagination and have fun!